The Garden Party &
The Fly

The Garden Party & The Fly

Level 500 Reader (H)

Katherine Mansfield

Doreen Lamb (Adaptor)
John McLean (Series Editor)

MATATABI PRESS

KATHERINE MANSFIELD

Katherine Mansfield
1888 - 1923

Katherine Mansfield Murry (née Beauchamp) was born in Thorndon, New Zealand in 1888. Her family were wealthy and influential.

In 1903, Katherine and her family moved to the UK. She attended Queens College, London, and developed an interest in writing. Upon graduation, she decided to pursue a career as a writer.

In 1911, Katherine published *In a German Pension*, a collection of thirteen short stories. From 1915 to 1917, she wrote numerous short stories, including *The Wind Blows* (1915), *Prelude* (1917), and *A Dill Pickle* (1917). She became known as a master of short stories.

In 1917, at the age of 29, Katherine developed tuberculosis. To get away from the cold winter in the UK, she moved to France. One of the most significant stories she wrote during her stay in France was *Je ne Parle pas Français* (1920) [I do not Speak French].

In 1921, Katherine travelled to Switzerland for medical treatment. Stories that she wrote in Switzerland include *The Doll's House* (1921), *The Garden Party* (1922), and her last story, *The Canary* (1923), in which a lonely woman describes her pet canary that has passed away.

In October 1922, Katherine returned to France. In January 1923, she died at the age of 34 after running up some stairs. She was buried in Avon.

First Published: September 2021

MATATABI PRESS (910554)
Windwhistle, Farley Hill, Matlock. DE4 3LL. UK
20-20, 5-Chome, Yamamoto-shinmachi, Asaminami-ku, Hiroshima.
731-0139. JAPAN
https://www.press.matatabi-japan.com/
https://www.holdings.matatabi-japan.com/
Email: press@matatabi-japan.com
Tel: 0081-(0)70-8592-2501

ACKNOWLEDGEMENTS

Special thanks are due to the students from the Department of English at Yasuda Women's University in Hiroshima, Japan. In the final editing stages, they diligently checked and tested the stories in this book to increase its suitability for EFL and ESL students worldwide.

CONTENTS

CONTENTS

THE GARDEN PARTY
— THE WORKMEN

The weather was perfect for a garden party. It was warm, the sky was blue, and the wind was gentle. The gardener had cut the grass. It shined in the early summer light. Hundreds of roses surrounded the garden like a picture frame.

Before breakfast, workmen arrived with a huge white tent. Meg opened a window to greet them. "Where do you want the tent, Miss?" one of the workmen asked.

Rose Garden [1]

"Mother, he wants to know where to put the tent," Meg said, turning around.

"Don't ask me, Darling. You children can decide everything this year. Pretend I'm not your mother. Pretend I'm a guest," she said, drinking her coffee.

Meg was wearing pyjamas. She had taken a morning shower and still had a towel on her head. "Mother, I can't go outside like this," she said, pointing at her head.

"Okay, Darling. Sit down and finish your breakfast. Laura, you're good at organizing things. Go outside, and tell the workmen where to put the tent."

Laura excitedly jumped up and ran into the garden. She had a piece of toast in her hand. She loved eating outside. "Food always tastes better when you eat it outside," she thought as she ran across the grass.

Four workmen were carefully putting the different parts of the tent onto the grass. They were wearing tool jackets.

Laura still had her toast in her hand. She looked around, but there was nowhere to put it. The workmen looked at her and smiled. "Workmen are so strong and handsome," she thought. Her face became a gentle red colour. She decided to talk to them like an adult. "Good morning, Men," she said, walking toward them.

A tall young man approached her. "Good morning, Miss," he said, smiling.

Laura started to feel nervous. "Oh, err, oh...the tent?" she said after a long pause.

"Yes, that's right, Miss," he said, taking off his hat. His eyes were warm and friendly. They were a beautiful dark blue colour. Laura breathed in deeply.

The other workmen took off their hats and approached. They were smiling, too. She breathed in deeply again. "It's a beautiful day," she thought, "and these workmen are *so* handsome and nice. How perfect!"

The tall young man spoke. "Where do you want the tent, Miss?" he said.

Laura looked around the garden. She pointed toward the lilies. "The lilies are beautiful at this time of the year," she said. "Can you put it next to the lilies?"

The workmen looked at the lilies. Then, they looked at one another. They shook their heads. A middle-aged man stepped forward.

Lily [2]

"Yes, the lilies are beautiful, Miss," he said in a rough voice. "However, if you put the tent there, nobody can see it from the road. Put it where it can be seen. It's huge. Everybody will be so jealous."

"Okay, how about on the tennis court, next to the band?" Laura suggested.

"A band?" the middle-aged man repeated. His hands were strong, and his eyes were dark. What was he thinking?

"It's a very small band," said Laura gently. "There's enough room for the tent, too."

Karaka Tree (New Zealand Laurel) [3]

The tall young man spoke. "How about over there, Miss?" he said, pointing toward the karaka trees. "That's the best place to put it."

Laura looked at the trees. "If the tent goes there, nobody can see the karaka trees," she thought.

"Their big shiny leaves and yellow fruit are so beautiful. Does it really need to go there?"

Before Laura could say what she was thinking, the three older workmen started carrying the tent toward the karaka trees. The young workman was still standing next to her. He was looking at a lavender bush. He gently touched it. Then, he put his fingers under his nose. He breathed in deeply. When Laura saw this, she stopped thinking about the karaka trees. She put her hands on her chest. "He's far more gentle and caring than all the middle-class boys I know," she thought. "Why can't I be friends with working-class men? Why can't I invite workmen to the house for dinner?"

Laura decided that it was wrong to separate people into working class, middle class, and upper class. "We're all the same," she though. "Class means nothing to me."

The workmen started putting up the tent. "Are you okay?" one said. "Let me help you," another said. The middle-aged workman began singing. The other men sang, too. They looked so happy working together. The tall young man ran to join them.

Laura felt so happy watching them. She felt like she was one of them. She felt like she was a work-girl.

"Laura, Laura, where are you?" Mother shouted from the house. "Telephone, Laura!"

"Coming!" she replied.

QUIZ (1)

1. What did the gardener do before breakfast?
2. What surrounded the garden like a picture frame?
3. When did the workmen arrive with the tent?
4. What did Meg do when the workmen arrived?
5. Why didn't Meg go outside to talk to the workmen?
6. What was Laura holding in her hand when she ran outside?
7. What were the workmen wearing?
8. Why do you think Laura's face became a gentle red colour when the workmen looked at her?
9. Describe the appearance of the young workman.

10. Why did Laura suggest putting the tent next to the lilies?
11. Why did the workmen disagree with Laura's suggestion?
12. Where did the young workman recommend putting the tent?
13. What kind of bush did the young workman gently touch?
14. What did Laura think it was wrong to do? Do you agree with her? Why / Why not?
15. Why did Laura return to the house?

THE GARDEN PARTY
— THE SONG

Laura ran across the grass, up the steps, and into the house. Her father and older brother, Laurie, were getting ready to go to the office.

"Laura," said Laurie, "my jacket's in the closet. I want to wear it to the garden party this afternoon. Can you tell the housekeeper to iron it for me?"

"Of course, I will," Laura said, running toward her older brother. She hugged him. "Oh, I love garden parties, don't you, Laurie?"

"I do, Laura. I really do," Laurie replied, warmly hugging his younger sister. He pointed toward the telephone. "Your friend, Kitty, is waiting."

Early 20th Century Telephone [4]

Laura answered the telephone. "Hello, Laura speaking," she said in a polite voice. "Oh, hi, Kitty. Thank you *so* much for phoning. The weather's beautiful, isn't it? Are you free this afternoon? We're having a small garden party...You are. Oh, excellent!"

"Laura! Laura!" Mother shouted from upstairs.

"Sorry, Kitty, please wait a minute. Mother's calling me." Laura gently put her hand over the mouthpiece. "What is it, Mother?" she shouted.

"Tell Kitty to wear that *beautiful* hat she wore last Sunday."

"Kitty, Mother says that you should wear that *beautiful* hat you wore last Sunday...Oh, you will. Excellent! See you at one o'clock. Bye-bye."

Laura breathed in deeply. "Ah, how wonderful," she said, breathing out. She sat on the floor and listened to all the sounds in the house. The doors and windows were open. The wind gently blew the curtains. Her sisters, Meg and Jose, were running from room to room upstairs, laughing. The workers were moving the piano into the living room. The sun gently shone through the windows.

The front doorbell rang. Sadie, the housekeeper, answered it. It was a man. He had something for the garden party.

Pink Lily [5]

Laura joined Sadie. "Who was it?" she asked.
"It was the man from the flower shop, Miss

Laura," she said, pointing toward the front door. "Look at these *beautiful* flowers."

There, just inside the front door, were twelve pots of pink lilies.

"Oh, my goodness, Sadie!" said Laura. "I've never seen so many lilies." She gently touched the lilies. "It must be a mistake, Sadie. Nobody buys this many lilies."

Mother joined them. "It's not a mistake," she said calmly. "I bought them. Aren't they lovely?" She touched Laura's arm. "I walked past the flower shop yesterday. They were in the window. I suddenly decided to buy all of them for the party."

Laura put her arms around her mother's neck. "Thank you so much, Mother," she said, hugging her.

The man from the flower shop rang the doorbell again. "More flowers, Miss," he said, putting six more pots of lilies next to the front door.

Hans and the other workers had finished moving the piano into the living room. Jose looked around the room. "Meg, let's put the chairs and the big leather sofa against the wall," she said. "Then, let's move everything else out of the room. What do you think?"

"Excellent idea," replied Meg.

"Hans, move these tables into the smoking room. Then, clean the floor. It's so dirty." Jose loved giving orders to the workers. "Oh, and one more thing, tell Mother and Laura to come here."

"Certainly, Miss Jose," said Hans.

Next, she looked at Meg. "I'm going to sing *This Life is Weary* at the garden party. Let's practise. You play the piano."

Meg looked at Jose. "Why do you want to sing a song about a broken heart and death?" she said, sitting down at the piano.

"Just play it, Meg," Jose said, smiling.

Mother and Laura entered the room. Meg started to play. *Pom! Ta-ta-ta Tee-ta!* A gentle sound filled the room. Jose put her hands together. She imagined that the man she loved had died. She pretended to wipe a tear from her eye. Then, she began.

This Life is Weary,
A Tear—a Sigh.

A Love that Changes,
This Life is Weary,
A Tear—a Sigh.
And then . . . Good-bye!

When she was singing the word *Good-bye*, her face changed. "Isn't my voice beautiful, Mother?" she said, smiling.

Before Mother could answer, Sadie entered the room. "Excuse me, Madam," she said.

"What is it, Sadie?"

"The cook wants the flags, Madam. Do you know where they are?"

"Flags? What flags?" Mother said, raising her hands.

"The paper flags for the sandwich table, Madam. The flags with the names of the sandwiches written on them."

Finally, Mother remembered. "Sadie, tell the cook to wait ten minutes," she said, pointing toward the kitchen.

Sadie went.

"Laura," Mother said quickly, "go into the

smoking room. I wrote the names of the sandwiches on a piece of paper. Find it!"

Laura jumped up and ran into the smoking room.

Mother looked at Meg and Jose. "Meg, take that towel off your head, and get dressed. You too, Jose, quickly, or I'll tell your father. Jose, after getting dressed, go into the kitchen. Talk nicely to the cook. She looks so angry today."

Laura found the piece of paper behind the clock. "Who put it there?" Mother said, taking it from Laura.

Mother read the sandwich names. Laura wrote them on the flags. "*Cream Cheese and Lemon*, *Egg and*...Laura, what is this? I need my glasses. It looks like *Egg and Mice*."

"It's olive, Mother," said Laura, looking at the piece of paper.

"Yes, of course, olive. *Egg and Olive*."

They finished writing the names. Laura took the flags into the kitchen. Jose was talking nicely to the cook. The cook wasn't angry.

"The sandwiches look *so* delicious, Cook," said

Jose in a warm and friendly voice. "How many different kinds did you make?"

"Fifteen, Miss Jose."

"Wow, that's amazing, Cook," Jose replied, gently touching the cook's shoulder.

The cook smiled.

"The cream cakes have arrived," said Sadie, pointing toward the window. A man from the cake shop was in the garden. He was holding a big box. It was full of cream cakes.

"Sadie, go outside and get the cakes," ordered the cook.

Sadie placed the cream cakes on the kitchen table. Laura and Jose looked at them. Cook started putting extra sugar on each one.

"Look at the cream cakes, Jose," said Laura. "They remind me of all of the parties we had when we were children."

Jose didn't like thinking about the past. "I guess so," she replied. "They do look delicious, don't they?"

"Have one," said the cook. "I won't tell your mother."

"No, we can't," said Jose. "We've just eaten

breakfast." Two minutes later, both Jose and Laura were licking cream off their fingers.

Laura took hold of Jose's hand. "Let's go into the garden," she said. I want to see if the workmen have finished putting up the tent. They're so handsome."

Sadie, Hans and the man from the cake shop were standing in front of the backdoor. Something had happened.

QUIZ (2)

1. What were Father and Laurie doing when Laura entered the house?
2. What did Laurie ask Laura to do? Why?
3. Why do you think Laura hugged Laurie?
4. What did Mother ask Kitty to wear?
5. What were Laura's sisters, Meg and Jose, doing when Laura was talking to Kitty on the telephone?
6. How many pots of lilies did the man from the flower shop bring to the house?
7. What did the worker, Hans, move into the living room?
8. Where did Jose tell Hans to put the tables?
9. What was the title of the song that Jose sang?
10. What was it about?

11. What did Mother forget to do?
12. Where was the piece of paper with the sandwich names?
13. Why couldn't Mother read the word *Olive*?
14. What didn't Jose like thinking about?
15. What do you think Laura wanted to show Jose in the garden?

5

THE GARDEN PARTY
— THE ACCIDENT

The man from the cake shop was explaining something very serious to Sadie and Hans. Sadie breathed in deeply and put both hands on her face. Hans shook his head. The cook joined them. "This isn't good," she said, turning toward Laura and Jose.

"What isn't good?" Laura nervously asked. "What's happened?"

"There's been a very bad accident," said Cook. "A man was killed."

"A man was killed! Where? How? When?" Laura said, looking around the garden.

The man from the cake shop spoke. "He lived in one of the small houses down the hill," he said.

"He was riding a big workhorse. It got scared and jumped up. He fell off and hit his head. Killed!"

Workhorse [6]

"Dead!" Laura said, shaking her head.

The man from the cake shop enjoyed telling everybody about the accident. "Dead!" he repeated. "He was young, too. He had a wife and five small children. His name was Mr. Scott."

"Jose, come here," said Laura. She held Jose's hand. They went into the living room. They were silent for a minute. Laura looked around the room.

"Jose!" she said, breathing quickly. "How can we stop everything?"

"Stop *everything*, Laura!" said Jose, shocked. "What do you mean?"

"Stop the garden party, of course."

"Stop the garden party?" Jose replied, shaking her head. "We can't do that. Nobody expects us to do that. Why do we have to stop the garden party?"

"We can't have a garden party. A neighbour was killed."

True, the small houses were nearby. You could see them from the front garden. However, they certainly weren't neighbours. You had to pass over a wide road to get to them. Workers and hundreds of children lived in them. They weren't nice houses. They were painted brown. Smoke came out of their dirty chimneys. The workers who lived in them used dirty language. Mother said the children must never go near the houses. She was worried they would start speaking like the workers.

"Think about the man's wife," said Laura. "She won't want to hear the band playing. She won't want to hear people singing and laughing."

"Oh, Laura!" Jose began to get angry. "You can't

stop a band playing every time somebody has an accident!" Her eyes became hard. "I feel sorry, too, but..." She looked directly at Laura. "The workers are always drinking alcohol. He was probably drunk. That's why he fell off the horse."

"Alcohol! Nobody said anything about alcohol." Laura started to feel angry. "I'm going to tell Mother what you said."

"Okay, go and tell Mother," Jose calmly replied.

Laura ran up the stairs. "Mother, can I come into your room?" she said, slowly opening the heavy door.

Mother was standing in front of a big mirror, trying on a new hat. "Of course, Darling," she replied. "Is everything okay? You look worried."

Early 20th Century Fashion [7]

"Mother, a man's been killed," Laura said, breathing quickly.

"In the garden?" Mother ran toward the window.

"No, no!"

"Oh, thank goodness! Laura, you shocked me!" Mother carefully removed her hat.

Laura told Mother about the accident and her conversation with Jose. "We have to cancel the party, don't we?" she said. "One of our neighbours has been killed!"

Mother quietly listened to Laura. Then, she stood up and walked toward the mirror. She picked up the hat again. "Laura," she said, "you only know about the accident because you were in the kitchen when the man from the cake shop arrived. Usually, nobody tells us when somebody from those dirty little houses dies. If you hadn't been in the kitchen, you would be getting ready for the party now, wouldn't you?"

Laura had to say *yes*, but it felt wrong. "Mother, isn't it bad to have a party?" she said.

Mother put her new hat on Laura's head. "Oh, how beautiful, Darling!" she said, stepping backward. "Look at yourself in the mirror. This hat is perfect for you."

Laura started to ask again. "Mother, isn't..."

"Stop talking about the accident, Laura," Mother coldly replied. "You'll make everybody feel bad. Those people don't expect us to cancel the party."

"I don't understand," said Laura, quickly walking out of the room. By chance, she saw herself in the mirror. She smiled. "Mother was right. I do look beautiful," she thought, turning from side to side in front of the mirror. She decided to think about the accident again after the party.

QUIZ (3)

1. What did Sadie do when she heard about the accident?
2. What did Hans do when he heard about the accident?
3. Where did the man who was killed in the accident live?
4. How did the accident happen?
5. Describe the family of the man who was killed.
6. Why do you think the man from the cake shop enjoyed telling everybody about the accident?
7. Laura said, "How can we stop everything?" What does *everything* refer to in this sentence?
8. Who lived in the small houses?

9. Describe the small houses.
10. Describe the language used by the workers who lived in the small houses.
11. Why did Laura get angry at Jose?
12. What was Mother doing when Laura entered her room?
13. What did Mother say Laura would be doing if she hadn't been in the kitchen when the man from the cake shop arrived?
14. Why did Mother get angry at Laura?
15. Why do you think Laura stopped thinking about the accident?

THE GARDEN PARTY
— THE PARTY

By one-thirty, the sandwiches and cream cakes were ready. At two o'clock, the band members arrived. They were wearing green jackets. Laura and her friend, Kitty, excitedly watched them get ready.

"Oh, Laura! How funny!" Kitty shouted. "They look like frogs. They should be playing music by the pond."

Jazz Band [8]

Laurie arrived home from the office. He waved to Laura and entered the house. Laura remembered the accident again. She wanted to tell Laurie about it. If Laurie says it's okay to have a party, it must be okay. "Laurie," she shouted, running toward the house.

Laurie was at the top of the stairs when she entered the house. "Hi, Laura!" he said, turning around. He opened his mouth wide. "Wow! You look *so* beautiful, and that hat is perfect."

Laura's face became a gentle red colour. "Is it?" she quietly replied, smiling at her older brother. She didn't tell him about the accident.

The guests started arriving, and the band started to play. The waiters ran from guest to guest with sandwiches, cakes, and drinks. There were so many guests. Some were looking at the flowers. Some were holding hands, and others were just walking around the garden. Everybody looked so happy. "How wonderful it is to be with happy people," Laura thought. "How wonderful it is to greet them, shake their hands, and look at their warm and happy eyes."

"Laura, Darling, you look so beautiful!" one guest said.

"That hat is so pretty!" another guest said.

"Laura, you look like a beautiful Spanish lady," another said.

Laura smiled widely and answered softly, "Would you like some tea? How about an ice cream? The passion-fruit ice cream is delicious."

Passion Fruit [9]

Father was talking to friends in the tent. "Father, shall I take some food and drinks to the band members?" Laura asked.

"Yes, Darling, please do that," he replied. "Thank you so much!"

After a perfect afternoon, the guests started to go home. "It was the best garden party ever..." "Perfect..." "The food was delicious..." "The band was wonderful..." they said.

Laura and Mother stood in front of the house. They thanked the guests for coming and waved goodbye. After some time, the last guests went home.

"What a wonderful party," said Mother. "Laura, let's have some fresh coffee. Tell the others to join us in the tent."

The family sat around a big table in the tent. The waiters brought coffee. "Have a sandwich, Father," Laura said. "I wrote the names on the flags."

"Thanks, Darling." Father quickly ate a sandwich. Then, he picked up another. "Did you hear about the accident?" he said.

"Darling," said Mother, breathing out strongly, "Laura told us about it again and again and again." She laughed. "She even wanted to cancel the party."

"Oh, Mother! Please don't be unkind to me," Laura said.

"It was very bad accident," Father said, putting his hand on Laura's shoulder. "The man was young. He was married and had five children, too. His house is just down the hill from here."

Everybody was silent.

QUIZ (4)

1. What was ready by one-thirty?
2. When did the band members arrive?
3. Who watched the band members get ready?
4. Why did Kitty say the band members looked like frogs?
5. What did Laurie do before entering the house?
6. What did Laura want to tell Laurie?
7. Did she tell him? Why do you think she did/ didn't tell him?
8. Why did Laurie open his mouth when he saw Laura?
9. What did the waiters give the guests?
10. What did Laura enjoy doing with the guests?

11. What kind of lady did one of the guests say Laura looked like?
12. What did Laura offer the guests?
13. What did Laura and Mother do in front of the house?
14. Where did the family drink coffee after the party?
15. Who spoke about the accident?

THE GARDEN PARTY
— THE BODY

Mother looked at the leftover sandwiches and cream cakes. She thought for a minute. Then, she smiled. "I know what we can do," she said. "Let's put the leftover food in a basket. We can give it to the dead man's wife and children."

Laura stood up. "Mother, we can't give them leftovers."

"Why not?" Mother replied. "We're not going to eat it. His children will love it. His wife can give some to the neighbours, too. Somebody, get me a big basket."

"But..." Laura started to say.

"Laura, what is wrong with you today? I

thought you wanted to do something nice for his family."

Oh well! Laura ran into the house. She came out with a basket.

Mother filled the basket with sandwiches and cream cakes. "Laura, take this food down the hill to the dead man's house," she said. "Take some pink lilies, too."

"Mother, not the lilies," Jose said, jumping up. "They'll make Laura's beautiful dress dirty."

"That's right! Just take the food." Mother followed Laura out of the tent. "Laura, don't..."

"Don't what, Mother?"

"Oh, nothing! Take care."

Laura walked down the hill toward the small houses. It was beginning to get dark. A big dog ran across the road. It stopped to look at Laura.

Working Dog [10]

The small houses were dark and quiet compared to the family home. Laura stood still for a minute. She tried to think about the man, the accident, and his dead body, but she couldn't. It felt unreal. The only thing she could think about was the party—the kisses, the voices, the laughter, and the smell of grass. She looked up at the sky, "Yes, it was a very successful party."

Laura arrived at the dead man's house. Children were playing on the road. Men and women were wearing dark coloured clothes. Laura's party dress and hat were very colourful. "I should have changed my clothes," she thought. "Maybe, I'll go home."

No, it's too late. This was the house. A group of people were standing in front of it. They stopped talking when they saw Laura.

Laura was very nervous. A woman was standing next to the front door. "Excuse me! Is this Ms. Scott's house?" Laura asked.

The woman smiled. "It is, Darling," she said.

Then, the door opened. Laura wanted to run home. "Help me, God," she said, looking into the house. A little woman dressed in black walked toward her.

"Are you Ms. Scott?" Laura said.

"Come in please, Miss," the woman said. She closed the door.

Laura looked at the door. She wanted to go home. "No," she said, "I don't want to come in. Please take this basket."

"Come this way, please, Miss," the woman said, walking into another room. Laura followed her. The room was dark. "A young lady is here," she said to a woman sitting on an old armchair. The woman slowly turned toward Laura. Her eyes were red. She was silent.

"Sorry about my sister," the little woman said. "It's been a long day."

"Please, please, don't trouble her. Take this basket. I want to go home."

The little woman opened another door. Laura walked through. It was the dead man's room. He was lying on a bed. A white bed sheet was over his face.

"Don't be afraid, Miss," she said in a soft voice. She slowly pulled the sheet from his face. "Come here, Miss."

Laura came. The young man looked like he was asleep, dreaming. His head was on a pillow, and his eyes were closed. He was peaceful. Never wake him up again. He was wonderful, beautiful. His sleeping face looked like it was saying, "Everything is okay. I am happy."

Laura didn't know what to say. She made a sound like a child crying. "I'm sorry," she said. "I should not be wearing this party hat."

She quickly left the house and silently walked past the people outside. It was dark.

Laurie was waiting on the road. He stepped forward. "Is that you, Laura?"

"Yes."

"Mother was worried. Are you okay?"

Laura held Laurie's arm. "Yes," she said, moving closer to him. "Oh, Laurie!"

"Are you crying?" he asked.

She was. Laurie put his hand on her shoulder. "Don't cry," he said in a warm, loving voice. "Was it really bad?"

"No," she said, crying. "It was wonderful. Laurie..." She looked at her brother. "Life is...Life is..." She couldn't explain.

Laurie understood. "It *is*, Laura. It *is*," he replied.

10

QUIZ (5)

1. What did Mother put in the basket for the dead man's family?
2. Do you think it was a good idea? Why? / Why not?
3. Who got the basket from the house?
4. Why didn't Laura take lilies to the dead man's family?
5. Mother said, "Laura, don't..." What do you think she was going to say?
6. What ran across the road in front of Laura?
7. Why couldn't Laura think about the man, the accident, and his dead body?
8. People were standing in front of the dead man's house. Describe their clothes.
9. Describe Laura's clothes.

10. Who was the woman who led Laura into the house?

11. What was the dead man's wife doing when Laura saw her?

12. What was on the dead man's face when Laura walked into the room?

13. What did Laura say when she saw the dead man?

14. Who was waiting outside for Laura?

15. Laura said, "It was wonderful." Why do you think she said this?

THE FLY — MR. WOOD

Armchair [11]

Old Mr. Wood sat down on a large, green,

leather armchair. "This is a very nice office, Boss," he said, gently moving his hand across the soft leather. The chair was so big that Wood looked like a small boy. It was time to go home, but he didn't want to leave. He wanted to stay in his old friend's office a little longer.

Last year, Wood suddenly became sick. He had to stop working. Now, his wife and daughters take care of him at home. He leaves the house once a week on Tuesdays. He goes into the city. His family didn't know what he did in the city. "He's probably causing problems for his old friends again," his wife always said after he left the house. Well, perhaps he was. We all need to do something that makes us feel happy.

The boss opened a small box. "Have a cigar, Wood," he said. He was five years older than Wood. He'd gained weight recently but was still strong and healthy. Wood always felt good after visiting him.

Wood smiled at his old boss. Then, he slowly looked around the office. "It's comfortable, really comfortable," he said, taking a cigar.

"Yes, it is comfortable," agreed the boss. He was

proud of his office. He liked it when people said nice things about it. "The workers were here last week," he explained. "New carpet," he said, pointing at the bright red carpet. "New bookcase, new table, and electric heating."

There was one thing that the boss did not want Wood to look at, a photograph. It wasn't new. It had been in the office for over six years. There was a young man in the photograph. He was wearing a uniform, and he had a serious look on his face. There were dark clouds in the sky above him.

"Boss, there was something I wanted to tell you," Wood said, looking up. "Now, what was it?" He touched his beard. "My head's not as good as it used to be." He breathed in deeply. His hand started to shake.

"Poor old man," thought the boss. "He'll probably die in a year or two." He opened one of the drawers in his desk. "Wood," he said, smiling warmly, "I've got something special." He took a bottle and two glasses out of the drawer. "One small glass of this will make you feel warm all day. It came from King George's castle."

Old Mr. Wood opened his mouth wide. "It's

whisky, isn't it?" he said. The boss showed him the bottle. It was whisky. "Boss, my wife never gives me whisky at home." He looked like he was going to cry.

The boss poured the whisky. "Drink it, Wood. It'll make you feel good. Don't put water in it."

Wood drank the whisky. He was silent for a minute. Then, he quietly said, "It tastes like nuts!"

"Excellent, Wood!

Wood started to feel warm. He also started to remember. "That's it!" he said, jumping up from the chair. "I remember what I wanted to tell you."

"Yes, what is it, Wood?"

"I went to Belgium last week with my wife and daughters. We went to my son's grave. He was killed there during The Great War." Wood looked at the boss. "We saw your son's grave, too. It was near to my son's."

Gravestones [12]
The Great War (1914 - 1918)

The boss was silent. He looked at the photograph on his desk.

"They take really good care of the graves, Boss," Wood continued. "Have you been to see your son's?"

"No, no!" For various reasons the boss had not been to see the grave.

"There were thousands and thousands of graves," Wood said. "They all had flowers growing on them. It looked like a beautiful garden."

Both men were silent.

Wood moved in his chair. "When you go there, be careful in the hotels," he suddenly said, laughing. "We were eating breakfast, and my wife asked for some jam. The waiter brought a small pot. It was about the size of my thumb. He asked her to pay ten francs for it—ten francs for one spoonful of jam. Well, she paid. She put the jam on her toast. Then, she put the pot in her bag. The waiter was surprised. He didn't expect her to keep the pot. They expect tourists pay for everything," he said, getting up and walking toward the door.

The boss laughed. "Yes, that's right!" he said, standing up. However, he didn't know what was *right*. He was thinking about something else.

The boss silently watched Wood leave the building. "If anybody comes, tell them I'm busy," he said to Macey, his secretary. "I don't want to speak to anybody for at least 30 minutes. Understand?"

"Certainly, Sir."

The door shut. The boss returned to his desk. He sat down on his chair and breathed out slowly. He put both hands on his face. He wanted to...he planned to cry...

12

QUIZ (6)

1. What did Mr. Wood look like when he was sitting on the large, green, leather armchair?
2. What happened to Wood last year?
3. Who did Wood live with?
4. How often did Wood leave the house?
5. What was in the small box?
6. What was new in the office?
7. Describe the man in the photograph.
8. Who was he?
9. What was in the bottle that the boss had in his desk drawer?
10. Where did it come from?
11. What did Wood say it tasted like?
12. When did Wood and his family go to Belgium?
13. What was near to Wood's son's grave?

14. What was growing on the graves?
15. What did the boss plan to do in his office for at least 30 minutes?

THE FLY — THE INKPOT

The boss felt shocked. Why did Wood speak about his son's grave? He imagined a big hole with his son's dead body in it. He imagined Wood, his wife, and his daughters looking at his son's dead body. It felt wrong. The boss did not want others to tell him that his son was dead in a grave. Six years had passed since The Great War, six years since his son was killed. He still wanted to imagine his son asleep, sleeping peacefully, not dead, not in a grave. "My son!" he yelled, putting both hands on his face...Nothing...No tears came. Why?

In the months and years after the boss's son was killed, he cried a lot. Sometimes, he cried so hard that his whole body shook. Just hearing his son's name made his eyes fill up with tears. People said that he would cry less as time passed by. "No, that will never happen," he thought. "He was my only son. I was going to give him my company. I worked so hard for so many years. I did it for him." Without his son, the company had no meaning. Without his son, life had no meaning.

In the year before The Great War, the boss and his son went to the office together every morning. His son learned about the company. He learned about the different jobs. He was intelligent, hardworking, and polite. The workers liked him. He smiled at them and said, "Excellent! How excellent!" However, that was in the past. That life and those dreams were in the past. Everything changed six years ago when a letter arrived. *We are very sorry to inform you that your son...*

"Six years passed so quickly," the boss thought. "It feels like he was killed yesterday." He lowered his hands from his face. "Why can't I cry?" Something was wrong. He decided to look at his son's photograph. It wasn't his favourite photograph. His son had a cold and serious look on his face. It was unnatural. He never looked like that.

Black Fly [13]

A black fly flew above the desk. It circled the boss and landed in the inkpot. After a minute, it tried to climb out. Its legs were heavy with ink. It fell backward into the ink and began to swim. The boss put his pen into the inkpot. The fly held on to it, and the boss gently lifted it out. He put it on a piece of paper. For a few seconds, the fly was still. The ink from its body turned the paper blue. Then, it moved its front legs. It slowly raised its body from the paper. It started the long and hard job of cleaning its body and wings. The boss watched. He was silent. After some time, the fly had finished. The danger was over. It had lived. Life could continue.

The boss looked at the fly. He had an idea. He put his pen in the inkpot. Then, he held it above the fly. Ink dropped onto the fly. "You didn't expect that, did you?" he said. "Well, what are you going to do now?"

The fly sat in a pool of ink. It slowly and painfully pulled itself forward. After a few seconds, it shook its front legs. Then, once again, it started the long and hard job of cleaning itself. "You're strong," the boss thought. He liked the way the fly got up and shook off the ink. "Don't lie down! Don't give up!" he said. "Don't ever give up!"

The fly finished cleaning. "Just one more time," the boss thought, putting his pen into the inkpot. Ink dropped onto the fly's back and wings. The boss watched in silence. The fly moved its front legs. "Well done! Well done!" he said. The fly was weak. The boss gently breathed on it. It was clean again.

The boss looked at his pen. He held it above the fly. Ink dropped onto the fly. "Come on," he said. Nothing happened. He waited. "Get up!" Nothing. The fly was dead.

The boss carefully picked up the fly, opened a window, and threw it out. He felt sad. He'd done something very bad. "Why?" he thought. "Macey, bring me some clean paper," he angrily shouted. "Quickly!"

The boss returned to his desk. "Now, what was I thinking about before that fly...?" he said to himself. "What was it?" It was gone. He could not remember.

QUIZ (7)

1. What did the boss imagine Wood, his wife, and daughters doing?
2. What did the boss want to imagine his son doing?
3. What did the boss do in the months and years after his son was killed?
4. What did the boss plan to give his son?
5. What had no meaning to the boss without his son?
6. What did the boss's son do in the year before The Great War?
7. Describe the boss's son.
8. What did the boss's son say to the workers?
9. What was written in the letter that the boss received?
10. Finish the sentence written in the letter.

11. What did the fly land in?
12. What did the boss do after the fly had finished cleaning itself?
13. What did the boss ask his secretary for?
14. What couldn't the boss remember?
15. Why do you think he couldn't remember?

ILLUSTRATIONS

1. Rose Garden: *Camille Pissarro (1862)*
2. Lily: *Sydenham Edwards (1806)*
3. Karaka Tree (New Zealand Laurel): *Sarah Featon (1848–1927)*
4. Early 20th Century Telephone: *Carol M. Highsmith*
5. Pink Lily: *Biodiversity Heritage Library*
6. Workhorse: *Jean Bernard (1816)*
7. Early 20th Century Fashion: *Otto Friedrich Carl Lendecke (1912)*
8. Jazz Band: *Peter Kuryla*
9. Passion Fruit: *Sarah Featon (1848–1927)*
10. Working Dog: *Kenneth McAlpine (1885)*
11. Armchair: *British Library*
12. Gravestones: *The Great War (1914 - 1918)*
13. Black Fly: *Fruit Grower's Guide*

KEY VOCABULARY

NOUNS

1. *Accident:* An unfortunate/sad occurrence
2. *Alcohol:* a strong liquid drunk by adults
3. *Armchair:* a chair with a place to put one's arms or elbows
4. *Band:* a group of musicians who perform together
5. *Basket:* a box-shaped container for carrying things
6. *Beard:* hair on a man's face
7. *Belgium:* a country on the north east border of France
8. *Chimney:* a passage above a fire for smoke (usually on top of a house)

9. *Cigar:* tobacco rolled in tobacco leaves (usually brown)

10. *Class:* a section of society (working class, middle class, upper class)

11. *Closet:* a room/space where clothes and/or personal items are kept

12. *Conversation:* two or more people talking to one another

13. *Darling:* a name used when talking to a loved one

14. *Drawer:* a box-shaped space in a desk or cabinet that can be opened

15. *Drunk:* the result of drinking too much alcohol

16. *Frame:* something used to display photos or paintings

17. *Francs:* money previously used in Belgium

18. *Gardener:* somebody who is paid to work in a garden

19. *Grave:* a place where a dead body is put

20. *Housekeeper:* somebody who is paid to work in a house

21. *Inkpot:* a pot containing ink for writing

22. ***King George V:*** the king of the United Kingdom from 1910 to 1936
23. ***Lavender bush:*** a bush with purple flowers that has a strong scent/smell
24. ***Leather:*** strong material made from animal skin
25. ***Leftovers:*** food remaining after everybody has finished eating
26. ***Mistake:*** something that is not correct
27. ***Mouthpiece:*** the part of the telephone that one talks into
28. ***Pond:*** a body of water that is smaller than a lake
29. ***Pyjamas (UK) Pajamas (US):*** clothes worn when sleeping
30. ***Secretary:*** a person who does general tasks in an office, such as taking notes, answering the telephone, and keeping records
31. ***Tool jacket:*** a jacket with many pockets for tools (hammers, screwdrivers...)
32. ***Tourist:*** someone visiting a town or city for pleasure (not work)
33. ***Uniform:*** clothes worn to show a person's job/position/status

34. *Upstairs:* the second/upper floor of a house or building

35. *Waiter:* a person who brings food to customers (usually in a restaurant)

VERBS

1. *Agree:* to have the same opinion/idea as somebody else

2. *Approach:* to move toward somebody/something

3. *Breathe:* to take air into or out from one's body

4. *Cancel:* to stop an event or activity

5. *Cause:* to make something happen (often negative)

6. *Circle:* to go/move around and around something

7. *Compare:* to look at similarities and differences between two or more things

8. *Expect:* to predict or think that something will happen

9. *Explain:* to give details above something

10. *Hug:* to put one's arms around somebody and hold them close

11. *Imagine:* to create an image, picture or story in one's head

12. *Inform:* to tell somebody about something

13. *Invite:* to ask somebody to come to an event or place

14. *Iron:* to use an iron to remove the creases from an item of clothing

15. *Land:* to come down from the air/sky to the ground

16. *Lick:* to touch something with one's tongue

17. *Order:* to tell somebody to do something

18. *Phone:* to contact/call someone using a telephone

19. *Practise (UK) Practice (US):* to do something to improve one's skill/ability

20. *Pretend:* to use the imagination to behave like somebody or something else

21. *Raise:* to move/lift something upward

22. *Remind:* to make a connection with a past memory

23. *Remove:* to take something off

24. *Separate:* to divide something into two or more groups/sections
25. *Shake:* to move something from side to side again and again
26. *Sigh:* to breathe out while making a sound (usually sad)
27. *Suggest:* to recommend doing something
28. *Surround:* to encircle (be on all sides)
29. *Wake:* to open one's eyes after sleeping
30. *Wave:* to move one's hand from side to side
31. *Yell:* to speak loudly

ADJECTIVES

1. *Afraid:* feel fear/scared
2. *Amazing:* impressive/great/wonderful
3. *Bright:* very light
4. *Broken:* to be damaged (not working)
5. *Comfortable:* pleasant/relaxing
6. *Dirty:* unclean/unpleasant
7. *Gentle:* soft/light/slight
8. *Handsome:* good-looking/attractive
9. *Huge:* very big

10. *Intelligent:* clever/knowledgeable
11. *Jealous:* envy/want something others have
12. *Nervous:* worried/uneasy/tense
13. *Polite:* speak nicely
14. *Proud:* feel happy about something / feel that something one has is special
15. *Rough:* not flat or smooth
16. *Scared:* feel fear/afraid
17. *Serious:* straight-faced/unsmiling
18. *Shocked:* surprised (usually by something negative)
19. *Surprised:* reaction to an unexpected event
20. *Unnatural:* different to usual
21. *Weary:* tired/sleepy/exhausted
22. *Wonderful:* great/amazing/special
23. *Worried:* uneasy/tense/nervous

INTERJECTIONS

1. *Excuse me:* something people say when they want somebody to listen to them
2. *Wow:* something people say when they feel surprised and/or impressed

QUIZ (1)

1. The gardener cut the grass before breakfast.
2. Roses surrounded the garden like a picture frame.
3. The workmen arrived with the tent before breakfast.
4. When the workmen arrived, Meg opened the window to greet them.
5. Meg didn't go outside to talk to the workmen because she was wearing pyjamas and had a towel on her head.
6. Laura was holding a piece of toast in her hand when she ran outside.
7. The workmen were wearing tool jackets.
8. Laura's face became a gentle red colour

when the workmen looked at her because...(answers vary)

9. The young workman was tall. His eyes were dark blue, warm, and friendly.

10. Laura suggested putting the tent next to the lilies because they were beautiful at that time of the year.

11. The workmen disagreed with Laura's suggestion about the tent because it could not be seen from the road.

12. The young workman recommended putting the tent next to the karaka trees.

13. The young workman gently touched a lavender bush.

14. Laura thought it was wrong to separate people by class. (Answers vary)

15. Laura returned to the house because she was wanted on the telephone.

QUIZ (2)

1. When Laura entered the house, Father and Laurie were getting ready to go to the office.

2. Laurie asked Laura to tell the housekeeper to iron his jacket because he wanted to wear it to the garden party.

3. (Answers vary)

4. Mother asked Kitty to wear the hat that she wore the previous Sunday.

5. When Laura was talking to Kitty on the telephone, her sisters, Meg and Jose, were running from room to room upstairs, laughing.

6. The man from the flower shop brought eighteen pots of lilies to the house.

7. Hans moved the piano into the living room.

8. Jose told Hans to put the tables in the smoking room.

9. The title of the song that Jose sang was *This Life is Weary*.

10. The song was about a broken heart and death.

11. Mother forget to write the names of the sandwiches on the flags.

12. The piece of paper with the sandwich names was behind the clock in the smoking room.

13. Mother couldn't read the word *Olive* because she wasn't wearing her glasses.

14. Jose didn't like thinking about the past.
15. (Answers vary)

QUIZ (3)

1. When Sadie heard about the accident, she breathed in deeply and put both hands on her face.
2. When Hans heard about the accident, he shook his head.
3. The man who was killed lived in one of the small houses down the hill.
4. The man fell off his big workhorse and hit his head.
5. The man who was killed was married with five small children.
6. (Answers vary)
7. *Everything* refers to the garden party and its preparations.
8. Workers and hundreds of children lived in the small houses.
9. The small houses were painted brown, and they had dirty chimneys.

10. The language used by the workers is referred to as dirty.

11. Laura got angry at Jose because Jose said that the man who died had been drinking alcohol.

12. When Laura entered Mother's room, she was standing in front of a big mirror, trying on a new hat.

13. Mother said that Laura would have been getting ready for the party if she hadn't been in the kitchen when the man from the cake shop arrived.

14. Mother got angry at Laura because talking about the accident would make everybody feel bad. Also, she believed that the workers didn't expect them to cancel the party.

15. Laura stopped thinking about the accident because she saw herself in the mirror, looking beautiful.

QUIZ (4)

1. By one-thirty, the sandwiches and cream cakes were ready.
2. The band members arrived at two o'clock.
3. Laura and Kitty watched the band members getting ready.
4. Kitty said the band members looked like frogs because they were wearing green jackets.
5. Laurie waved to Laura before entering the house.
6. Laura wanted to tell Laurie about the accident.
7. No, she didn't tell him. (Answers vary)
8. Laurie opened his mouth when he saw Laura because he was surprised by how beautiful she looked.
9. The waiters gave the guests sandwiches, cakes and drinks.
10. Laura enjoyed greeting the guests, shaking their hands, and looking at their warm and happy eyes.
11. One guest said that Laura looked like a beautiful Spanish lady.
12. Laura offered the guests tea and ice-cream.

13. Laura and Mother thanked the guests and waved goodbye to them in front of the house.
14. The family drank coffee in the tent after the party.
15. Father spoke about the accident.

QUIZ (5)

1. Mother put the leftover sandwiches and cakes in the basket for the dead man's family.
2. (Answers vary)
3. Laura got the basket from the house.
4. Laura didn't take lilies to the dead man's family because they would make her dress dirty.
5. (Answers vary)
6. A big dog ran across the road in front of Laura.
7. Laura couldn't think about the man, the accident, and his dead body because she was thinking about the party.
8. The people who were standing in front of

the dead man's house were wearing dark coloured clothes.

9. Laura was wearing a colourful party dress and hat.

10. The dead man's wife's sister (sister-in-law) led Laura into the house.

11. When Laura saw the dead man's wife, she was sitting on an old armchair.

12. A white bed sheet was on the dead man's face when Laura walked into the room

13. When Laura saw the dead man, she said, "I'm sorry. I should not be wearing this party hat."

14. Laurie was waiting outside for Laura.

15. (Answers vary)

QUIZ (6)

1. Wood looked like a small boy when he was sitting on the large, green, leather armchair.

2. Last year, Wood suddenly became sick and had to stop working.

3. Wood lived with his wife and daughters.

4. Wood left the house once a week on Tuesdays.

5. Cigars were in the small box.

6. The carpet, bookcase, table and electric heating were new in the office.

7. The man in the photograph was young. He was wearing a uniform and had a serious look on his face.

8. He was the boss's son.

9. Whisky was in the bottle that the boss had in his desk drawer.

10. The whisky was from King George's castle.

11. Wood said the whisky tasted like nuts.

12. Wood and his family went to Belgium last week.

13. The boss's son's grave was near to Wood's son's grave.

14. Flowers were growing on the graves.

15. The boss planned to cry in his office for at least 30 minutes.

QUIZ (7)

1. The boss imagined Wood, his wife, and daughters looking at his son in a grave.
2. The boss wanted to imagine his son asleep, sleeping peacefully.
3. In the months and years after his son was killed, the boss cried a lot.
4. The boss planned to give his son his company.
5. The boss's company and life had no meaning without his son.
6. In the year before The Great War, the boss's son learned about the company and the different jobs.
7. The boss's son was intelligent, hardworking, and polite.
8. The boss's son said, "Excellent! How excellent!" to the workers.
9. *We are very sorry to inform you that your son...* was written in the letter that the boss received.
10. *We are very sorry to inform you that your son has been killed.*
11. The fly landed in the inkpot.

12. The boss dropped ink onto the fly after it had finished cleaning.
13. The boss asked his secretary for some clean paper.
14. The boss couldn't remember that he was thinking about his son.
15. (Answers vary)

NOTE FROM THE PUBLISHER

At MATATABI PRESS, we're always looking for new talent. Contact us at the email, below, if:

1. You're a writer with a story to tell;
2. You're an EFL/ESL professional interested in working on an English graded reader;
3. You're a Japanese language specialist interested in working on a Japanese graded reader; or
4. You're a Japanese-English translator interested in translating one of our publications.

Email: press@matatabi-japan.com
https://www.press.matatabi-japan.com/

Matatabi Readers are graded by *sentence complexity* and *headword count*.

Sentence Complexity

Sentence Complexity Level	Flesch-Kincaid Grade Level
400	1 to 2
500	2 to 3
600	3 to 4
700	4 to 5
800	5 to 6
900	6 to 7
1000	7 to 8
1100	8 to 9
1200	9 to 10
1300+	10+

Sentence complexity is calculated using the Flesch-Kincaid Grade Level Formula. Grade Level "3 to 4" (Level 600), for example, indicates that the sentence complexity is suitable for students in the third and/or fourth grade of school in the U.S.

Headword Count

Headword Level	Headword Count
D	301 to 400
E	401 to 500
F	501 to 600
G	601 to 700
H	701 to 800
I	801 to 900
J	901 to 1000
K	1001 to 1100
L+	1101+

The headword count in a Matatabi Reader represents the number of words with separate definitions. Even if a word, such as *ship*, appears on every page in a book, it only represents one headword. Likewise, verbs, adjectives, and nouns in all their forms are counted as single headwords. For example:

1. Eat, ate, eaten, and eating represent one headword;
2. Tall, taller, and tallest represent one headword; and
3. Cake and cakes represent one headword.

MATATABI TRANSLATION SERVICES
https://www.translate.matatabi-japan.com/

English Editing
(edit@matatabi-japan.com)

Essays, Research Articles, MA Theses, Doctoral Theses, Conference Presentations, Business Emails, Sound Files, Websites, Materials for Publication...

Japanese-to-English Translation
(translate@matatabi-japan.com)

Film Subtitles / Audio Visual Translation (SRT, DFXP, SBV,SSA, TXT, VTT), Business Emails, Essays, Research Articles, Conference Presentations, Websites, Picture Books, Materials for Publication...

EDITORS

Doreen Lamb (Adaptor)

Doreen is an experienced English copyeditor and proofreader. She is based in the UK and is interested in feminist literature and stories for young learners.

John McLean (Series Editor)

John is an associate professor at Yasuda Women's University in Hiroshima, Japan. He oversees the Department of English Interpreting Stream. He is known for his interpreting work with some of Japan's leading athletes and film directors. In 2020, he subtitled Toshihiro Goto's award winning film "Hiroshima Piano" [*Okasan no Hibaku Piano*].

CPSIA information can be obtained
at www.ICGtesting.com
Printed in the USA
BVHW052120100723
667055BV00006B/237